A Troll First-Start® Tall Tale

Paul Bunyan

AND HIS BLUE OX

by Patsy Jensen • illustrated by Jean Pidgeon

Troll Associates

Paul Bunyan is one of the most famous American folk heroes. According to the stories told about him, he used his incredible strength to build such sights as the Rocky Mountains and the Mississippi River.

A tall tale is an unusual story that has been exaggerated as it is retold over the years. Although no one person could ever do the kinds of things attributed to Paul Bunyan, we can believe in his spirit and determination to succeed.

Paul Bunyan was the biggest and best lumberjack who ever lived.

It is said that Paul was born in Maine, but no one really knows for sure. What we do know is that Paul was a very large baby. He weighed 86 pounds when he was born.

Paul's appetite matched his size. One day he ate 74 buckets of oatmeal and drank 14 gallons of milk. And that was just for breakfast!

Paul grew so quickly that his mother had to make him a new set of clothes every week.

And legend has it that Paul did not wear shoes until he was fully grown. Before that he simply wore sheets for socks, and barrels for shoes.

When he was still very young, Paul left
his parents' farm to seek his fortune. Since
he loved the outdoors, Paul decided to
become a logger.

Paul took a job at the first logging camp he visited.

One of Paul's favorite chores was that of daybreaker. Paul would head up into the mountains with a big ax to break day and start the morning.

Of course, Paul's ax was biggest of all!
The handle was made of a whole hickory tree,
and the blade was the size of a barn door.

Paul quickly became known as the best logger in camp. But one day he decided to move on to new adventures.

When Paul started out, the Winter of the Blue Snow began. Blue snow fell day after day.

One day, Paul tripped over something. Suddenly he saw a most unusual sight.

Sticking out of a snow drift were two huge, hairy ears!

Naturally, Paul was very curious.
He pulled on the ears as hard as he could.
And what should come out but a baby
blue ox!

This baby was the largest animal Paul
had ever seen. His arms shook when he
lifted it.

Paul rushed home with the little ox and covered it with blankets. Soon the ox stood up and licked Paul's hand with its tongue.

"Babe, we'll be great friends!" Paul said happily.

Soon Paul and Babe were working side by side. Paul chopped down the trees. Babe hauled them wherever they needed to go.

Babe grew and grew. Although there were no scales around to weigh the ox, Paul measured the distance between Babe's eyes. It came to 42 ax handles, give or take a handle.

After a time Paul decided to start his own logging camp. He wanted to make it the biggest logging camp ever.

Paul knew he would need plenty of water for such a huge camp. That's when he dug the Great Lakes.

The camp was so large that the workers needed compasses and maps to get around. Many workers got lost. A few were never found.

24

The cookhouse alone covered four square miles. Paul's favorite meal was pancakes. A pipeline was built to bring the syrup right to his table.

Word about Paul's strength spread around the country. Soon he was asked to help out in other places.

Once Paul dug a canal in the middle of the country. While he was digging, he threw dirt to his right and to his left.

One pile of dirt became the Rocky Mountains. The other became the Appalachian Mountains. When Babe kicked over a bucket of water to fill it, he made the Mississippi River.

One time Babe was called upon to straighten a crooked road.

Paul hitched Babe to the end of the road. The big ox pulled and pulled. Soon there was a loud CRACK! When things got quiet, the road was perfectly straight.

After their adventures, Paul and Babe
always headed back to camp.

Where is Paul Bunyan today? No one really knows. One day he and Babe just headed into the woods and were never heard from again. But if you're ever walking in the forest and hear the cry of "Timber!", don't be surprised if you see a great man and his big, blue ox just around the bend.